Trumpet

Guiro

Saxophone

Tambourine

Guitar

Flute

Violin

Castanets

Chimes

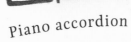

Bassoon

Piano accordion

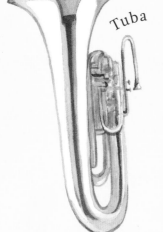

Tuba

Kettledrum

For
Charlie and Jayme's great-grandfather, Tommy Jones —N.R.

Nina Rycroft used watercolor, gouache, and colored pencil
for the illustrations in this book.

Library of Congress Cataloging-in-Publication Data

Harris, Stephen, 1959–
Ballroom bonanza : a hidden pictures ABC book / by Stephen Harris and Nina Rycroft ; illustrated by Nina Rycroft.
p. cm.
Summary: Animals from alpacas to zebras gather in Blackpool for the annual dance competition, while the monkeys
hide twenty-six musical instruments, which the reader is invited to search for in the illustrations.
ISBN 978-0-8109-8842-2
[1. Stories in rhyme. 2. Dance—Fiction. 3. Balls (Parties)—Fiction. 4. Animals—Fiction. 5. Alphabet. 6. Counting.
7. Picture puzzles.] I. Rycroft, Nina, ill. II. Title.
PZ8.3.H24316Bal 2010
[E]—dc22
2009016537

Concept by Nina Rycroft
Text copyright © Stephen Harris 2009
Illustrations copyright © Nina Rycroft 2009

Printed and bound in China
10 9 8 7 6 5 4 3 2 1

Abrams Books for Young Readers are available at special discounts when purchased in quantity for premiums and
promotions as well as fundraising or educational use. Special editions can also be created to specification. For details,
contact specialmarkets@abramsbooks.com or the address below.

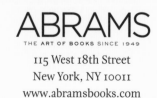

THE ART OF BOOKS SINCE 1949
115 West 18th Street
New York, NY 10011
www.abramsbooks.com

BALLROOM BONANZA

Concept and Illustrations by
Nina Rycroft

Story by
Nina Rycroft AND Stephen Harris

Abrams Books for Young Readers
New York

In the famous town of Blackpool,
Each October, you will find
Gathered in the Tower Ballroom
Animals of every kind.

It's a dancing competition.
Who will win the prize this year?
Let us watch as keen contenders
Alphabetically appear.

Aa First, the affluent alpacas
All arrive, superbly dressed.

Bb Then the bears in bright boleros.
(Everyone is most impressed.)

C c On the floor the camels conga
In the latest Latin style.

Dd Donkeys demonstrate the disco.
(This can last for quite a while.)

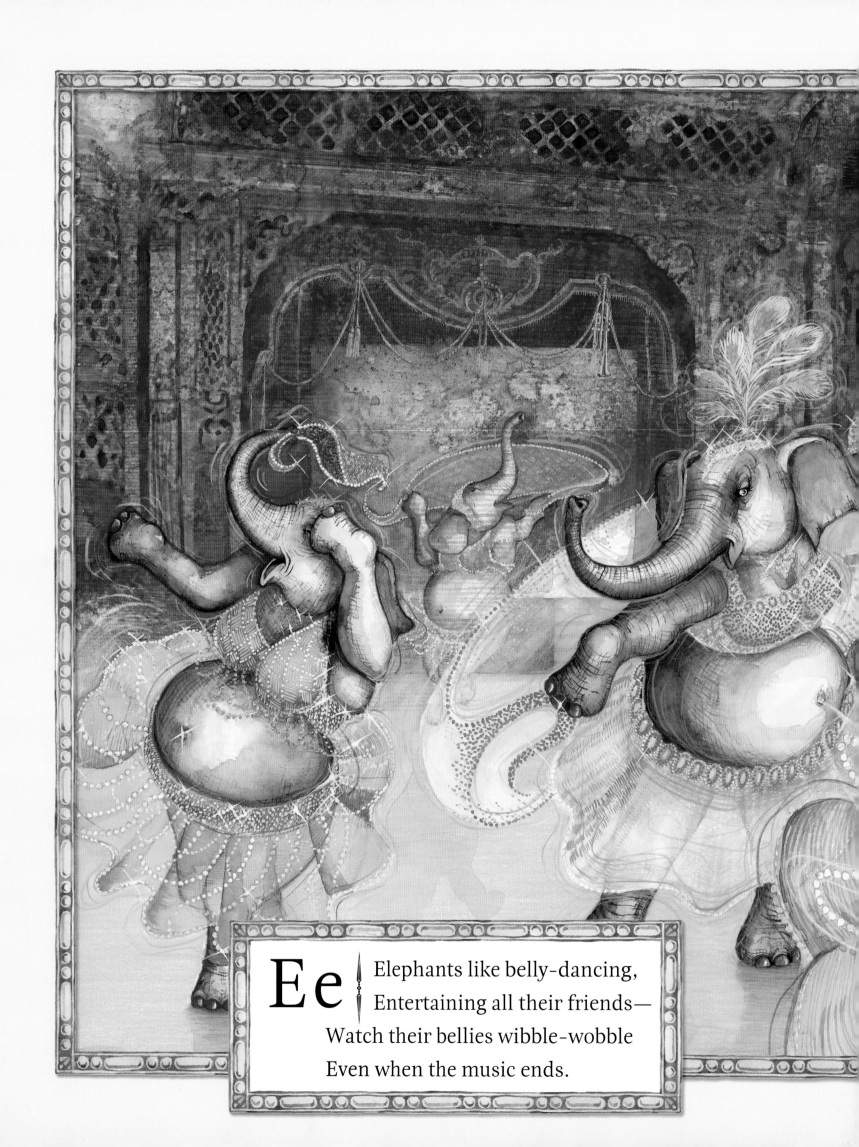

Ee
Elephants like belly-dancing,
Entertaining all their friends—
Watch their bellies wibble-wobble
Even when the music ends.

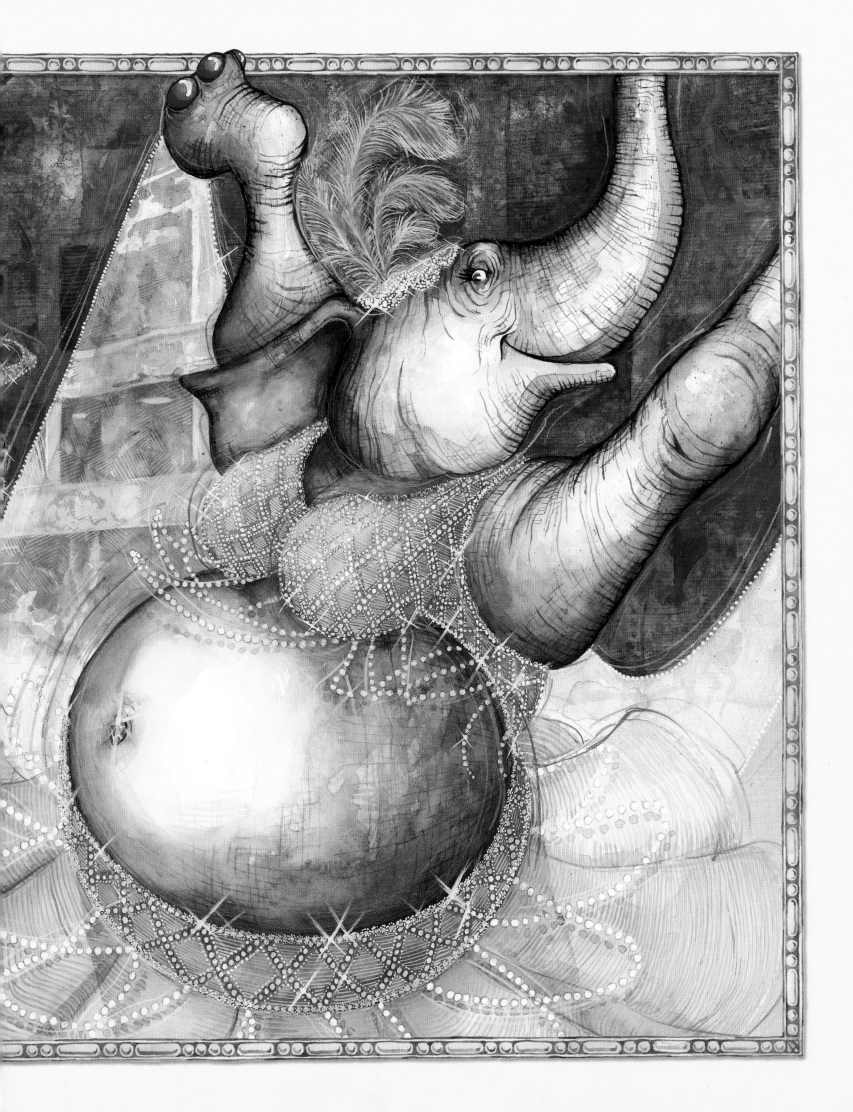

Ff | When flamingos dance flamenco,
Judges have to block their ears.

G g Groovy goats try go-go dancing.
(No one's laughed as much in years.)

Hh

Here we have the hefty hippos.
Happily their hooves they pound,
Heaving to the latest hip-hop
With their hats the wrong way round.

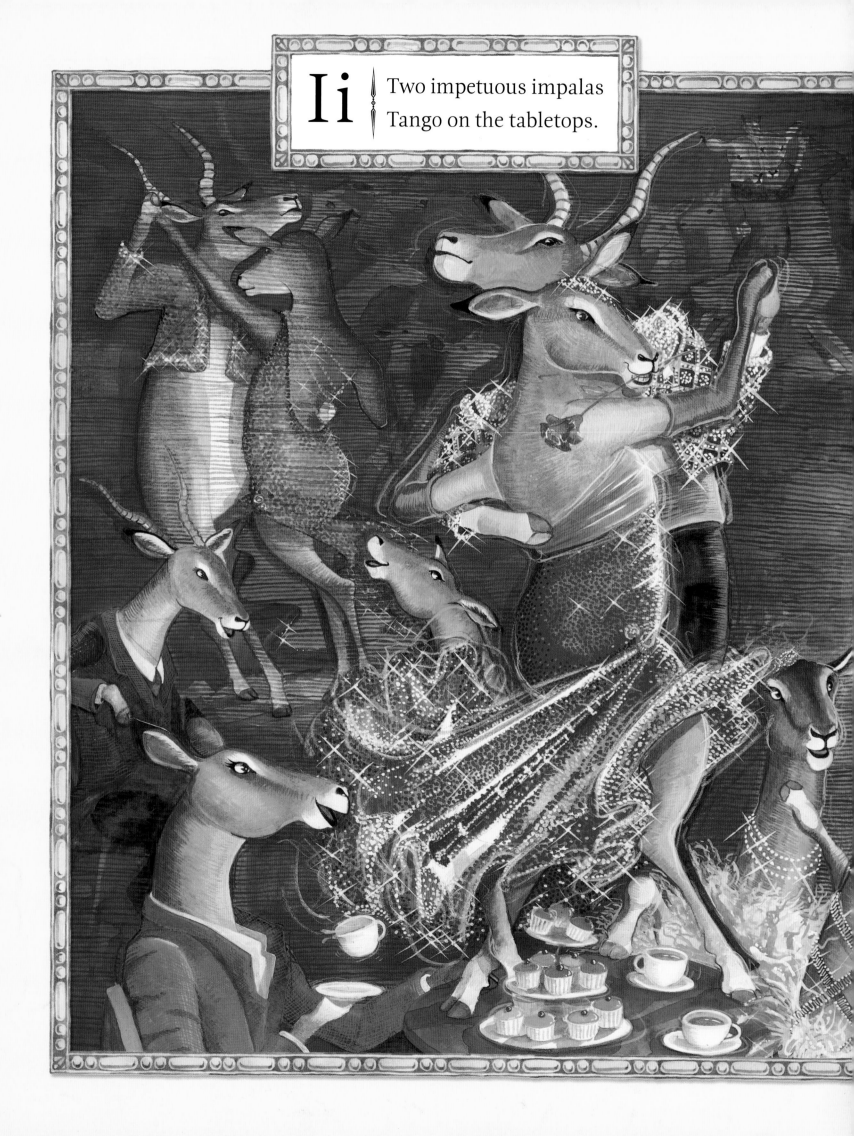

Ii

Two impetuous impalas
Tango on the tabletops.

Jj Next, a jaguar who jetés
Blushes as her tutu drops.

Kk   Kangaroos are keen on cancan—
Such a night they'd never miss.

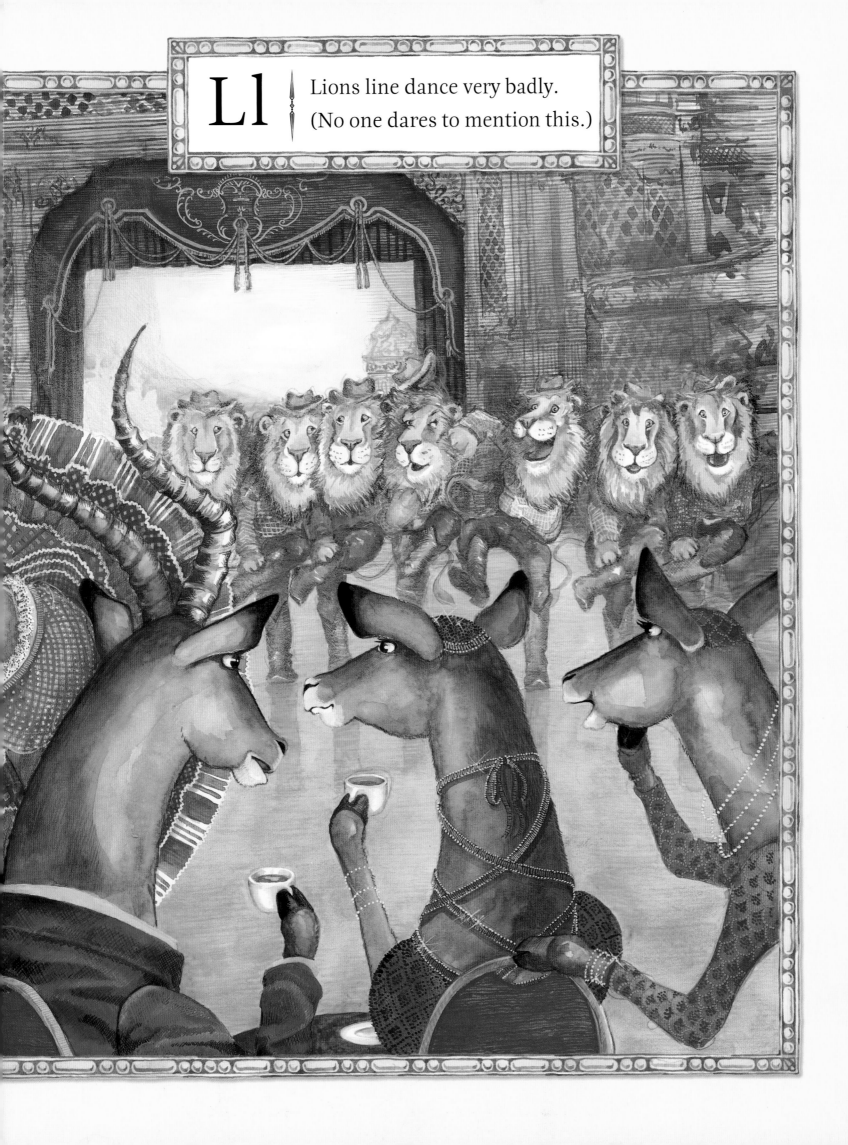

Ll Lions line dance very badly.
(No one dares to mention this.)

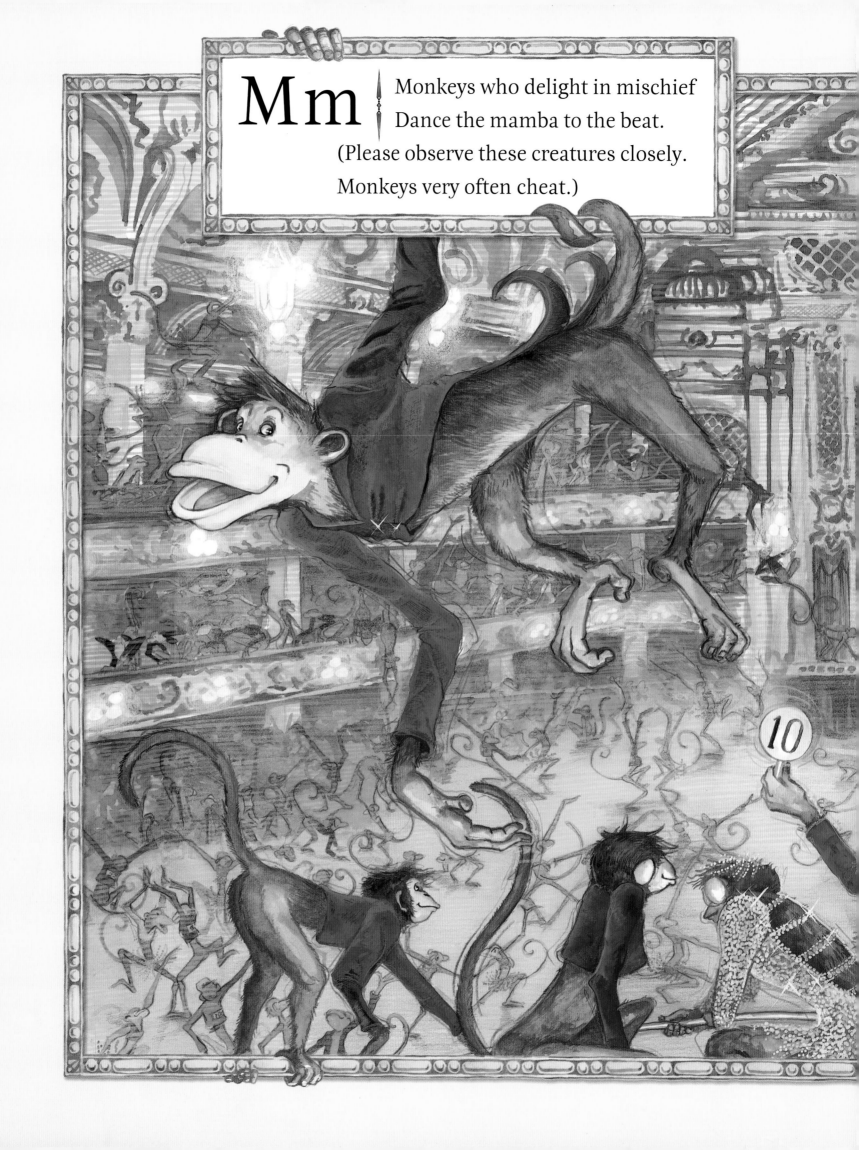

Mm Monkeys who delight in mischief
Dance the mamba to the beat.
(Please observe these creatures closely.
Monkeys very often cheat.)

N n Numbats nimbly do the Nutbush
(Not a clever dance, it's true).

Oo   Followed by orangutans
Who bop and do the boogaloo.

P p Penguins proudly take their partners,
Then the polka they present.

Q q Quails dance a quaint quadrille
And question where those monkeys went.

R r When the rhinos do the rumba,
No one can believe their eyes.
Hardly anything is broken,
Much to everyone's surprise.

S s | Sassy swans perform the samba,
Shaking tail feathers white.

T t | Turkeys do the twist, and ponder
What the monkeys plan tonight.

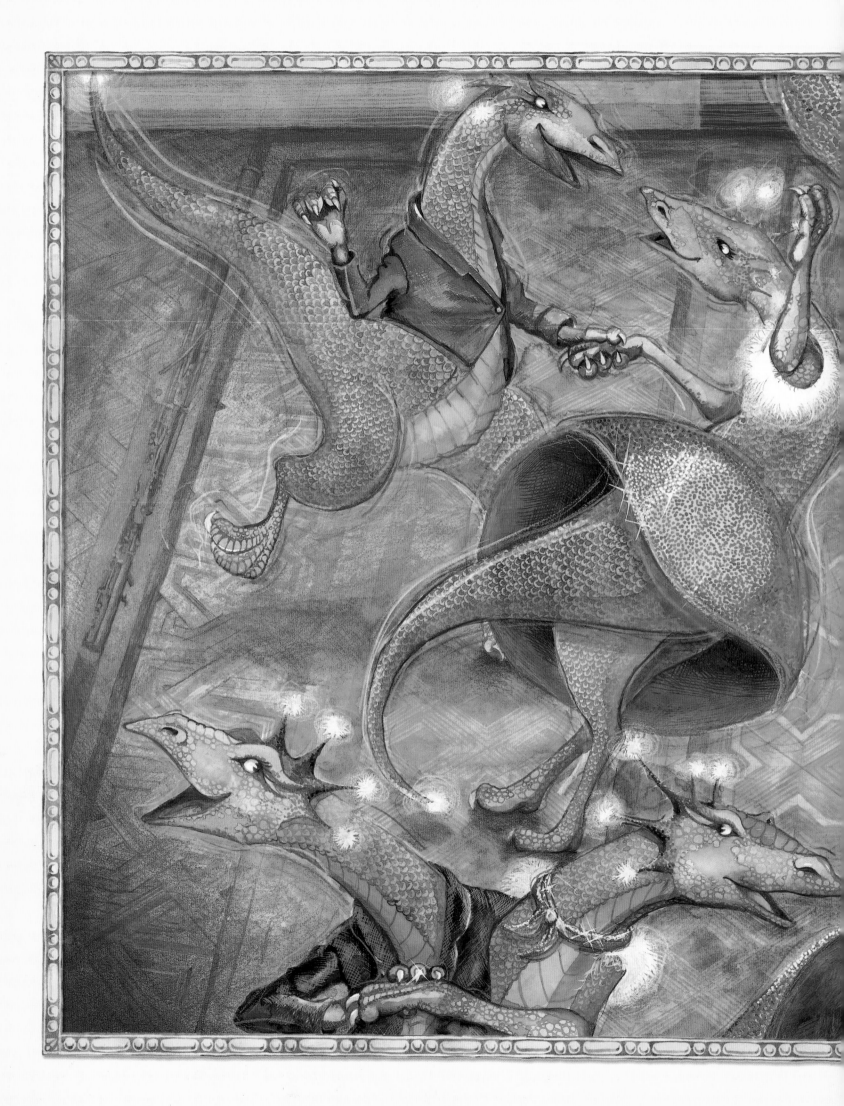

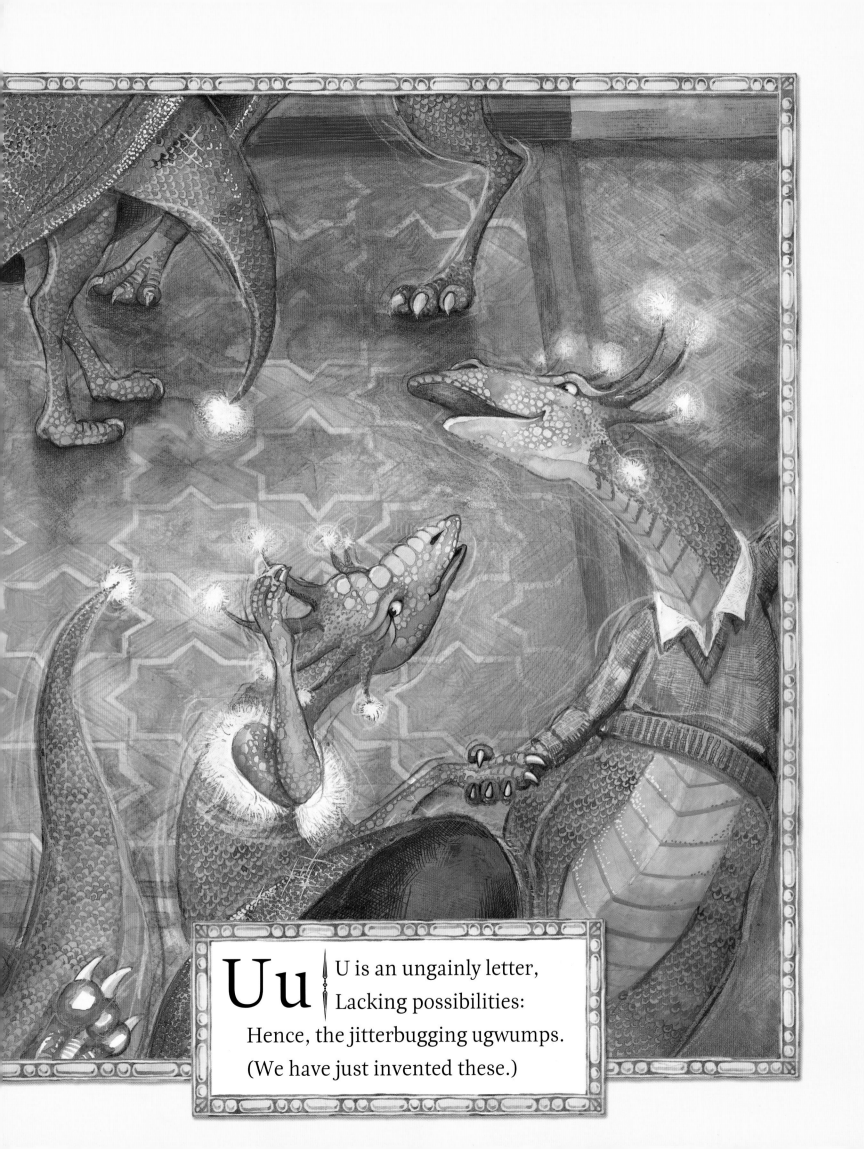

U u
U is an ungainly letter,
Lacking possibilities:
Hence, the jitterbugging ugwumps.
(We have just invented these.)

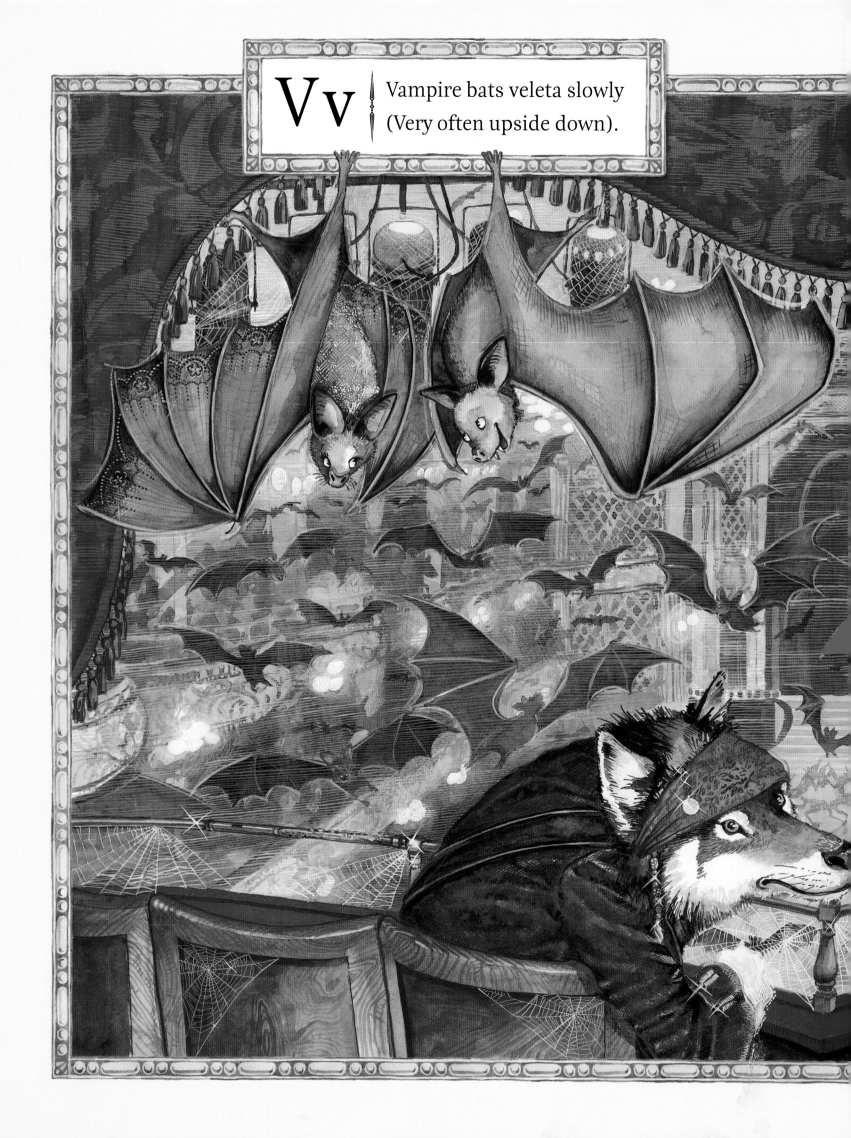

V v Vampire bats veleta slowly
(Very often upside down).

Ww
Wolves and wolverines watusi,
Wailing till they wake the town.

Xx Oxen foxtrot extra-quickly—
Such an excellent display!

Yy Yaks enjoy the hootchy-kootchy
In a hurly-burly kind of way.

Zz Last of all, we have the zebras,
Putting on a ritzy show.
They can dance the zapateado.
(No one can pronounce it, though.)

Judges try to pick a winner
In a manner just and fair.
Finding that it's far from easy,
"All are winners!" they declare.

After that, the grand finale.
Dancers ask the band to play.
"Sorry, but those naughty monkeys
Hid our instruments!" they say.

Check each page from A to Z, now.
Prove you're good at monkey tricks!
Find the hidden instruments.
(In total, there are twenty-six.)

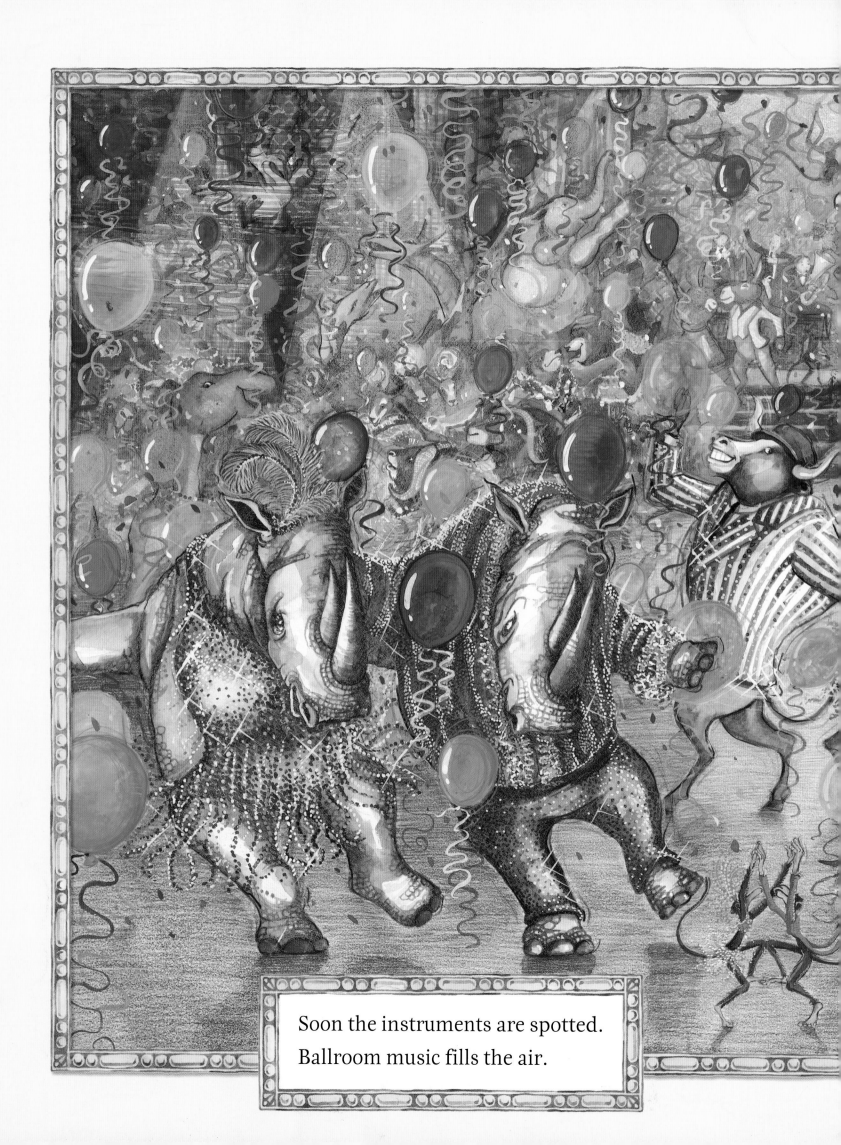

Soon the instruments are spotted.
Ballroom music fills the air.

Jiving, flinging, stomping, swinging
Animals are everywhere.

Dreamily they leave the ballroom
Just as dawn is drawing near.
Everybody makes a promise:
"See you all again next year."

The Mystery of the Missing Musical Instruments

Where did those mischievous monkeys hide the orchestra's musical instruments?
Look at the instruments on the endpapers and then try to find them on each of the twenty-six
illustrations featuring a letter of the alphabet. The answers are below.

———◆———

Answers

A: Xylophone (ceiling); **B:** Harp (stairway); **C:** Maracas (headdress);
D: Castanets (floor lights); **E:** Trumpet (curtain tassel); **F:** Tuba (trophy);
G: Chimes (balcony column); **H:** French horn (stage—right); **I:** Clarinet (dress);
J: Triangle (floor); **K:** Snare drum (balcony); **L:** Guitar (stage—top);
M: Kettledrum (light); **N:** Güiro (shadow—arm); **O:** Tambourine (hat); **P:** Flute (stair);
Q: Cello (shadow—floor); **R:** Trombone (space between rhinos in foreground);
S: Saxophone (swan's neck); **T:** Piano accordion (ceiling); **U:** Bassoon (floor pattern);
V: Piccolo (railing); **W:** Violin (spotlight); **X:** Banjo (stage—left); **Y:** Cymbals (jacket);
Z: Contrabassoon (space between zebras on right).

Xylophone

Banjo

Snare drum

Cello

Maracas

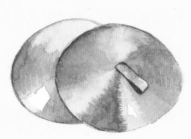

Triangle

Clarinet

French horn

Contrabassoon

Piccolo

Harp

Cymbals

Trombone

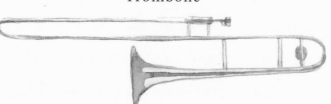